Disney

SNEAKERELLA

IF THE SNEAKER FITS

TELEPLAY BY DAVID LIGHT & JOSEPH RASO AND TAMARA CHESTNA AND MINDY STERN & GEORGE GORE II

ADAPTED BY ANNIE AUERBACH

DISNEP PRESS

LOS ANGELES • NEW YORK

El is from Queens, New York.
He lives with his stepfather
and stepbrothers.

They live above the shoe store
they own.
El's dream is to design sneakers.
Sami is his best friend.
She wants to help make El's dream
come true.

El and Sami get in line at the King6 shoe store.

They want to get the newest sneakers.

They meet Kira.

El takes Kira on a tour of Queens.

He thinks Queens is the best ever.

He shows her all his
favorite places.
Kira tries the tasty food in
El's neighborhood.

El takes her to the community garden.
He gives her a flower.

Soon Kira agrees.
It *is* the best ever!

Before Kira can tell El who she is,
El has to get back to the store.
He was supposed to be working all
this time.
El gets in trouble with his
stepfather, Trey.

El learns that Trey is going to sell the store!

That makes El sad.

His mother started the store.

He still misses her.

She taught him to make sneakers.

Kira goes home to her penthouse.

Her father is Darius King.

He is famous for his sneaker designs.

Kira tells her father that he should
bring in a new shoe designer.
He asks her to help find someone.
She knows she has an important
task now.

The next day, El learns who Kira is.
He can't believe it.

Sami has a plan.
She tells El to design some new
kicks to show Kira who he really is.

They can show her at Kira's family's
charity gala.

El works hard
to make a new
sneaker.
He knows it will
have to be his
best work ever.

El finishes a one-of-a-kind shoe. But on the night of the gala, his stepbrothers take his phone.

They lock El in the stockroom.

Suddenly, the door flies open.
It's Gustavo!
He is El's friend from
the neighborhood.
He lets out El.

Gustavo uses a little magic to get
nice clothes for El and Sami.
Then he loans them an orange car.
Gustavo tells them they must be
done by midnight.
After that, the spell will fade away.

El finds Kira at the gala.
They dance.

Kira wants El to meet her father.
She tells El that he could design
for the King brand.
El can't believe it.

Kira asks if El has designed for
other people.
He doesn't want to let her down.
So he lies to her.

The clock begins to strike midnight.
El rushes to leave.
Kira and her sister, Liv, are confused.
El trips and leaves a sneaker behind.

Kira has the sneaker El left at
the gala.
She shows it to her father.
He is impressed.
But Kira has no way to find El.

So Kira and Liv come up with a plan to find him.

Liv posts a message on the Internet. She calls it #WheresMyPrince.

Kira and Liv do a photo shoot.
Kira receives lots of messages.
They are not about the right sneaker.
They are not from the right guy.
They are not from El.

Finally, El sends a photo to Kira.
It is of the matching sneaker.
Kira tells him to come meet with
her father.
El and Sami celebrate.

El's stepbrothers steal the sneaker.
Then they meet with King.
They reveal that El is just a stock boy.

King is not happy that El lied.
Kira is not happy, either.

El wants to make things right
with Kira.

He goes to SneakerCon to see her.

El tells Kira he is sorry.

He tells King he is sorry.

Kira forgives him.

So does King.

King suggests that he and El
be partners.

El's dream has come true!

One year later, everything is perfect.
El has his own sneaker brand.
Everybody loves his kicks—
especially Kira!